THE JOKER'S JOKE BOOK

By
MORT TODD
Illustrated by
JOEY CAVALIERI

TOR

A TOM DOHERTY ASSOCIATES BOOK

This is a work of fiction. All the characters and events
portrayed in this book are fictional, and any resemblance to
real people or incidents is purely coincidental.

THE JOKER™'S JOKE BOOK

First printing: September 1988

A TOR BOOK

Published by Tom Doherty Associates Inc.
49 West 24th Street
New York, NY 10010

ISBN: 0-812-57125-8
CAN. ED.: 0-812-57126-6

Printed in the United States of America

What does the Joker create every day?
A nuisance out of himself!

What did the grape say when the Joker stepped on it?
Nothing . . . it just let out a little wine!

Why did the Joker steal only pennies?
He thought some change would do him good!

Why did the Joker try to see the President about some furniture?
Because he heard the President was a cabinet maker!

Is the Joker animal, vegetable or mineral?
Vegetable . . . he's a human bean!

Why does Batman think the Joker is like the Internal Revenue Service?
They've both been taxing him for years!

Why did the Joker carry a large handkerchief?
For crying out loud!

Why did the Joker stand in front of a mirror with his eyes closed?
To see what he would look like when he was asleep!

Why does the Joker wish he could be a guitar player in a room full of beautiful girls?
Because if he was a guitar player, he would have his pick!

What happened when Bruce Wayne's thoroughbred colt whinnied too much?
It became hoarse!

What's the Joker's definition of "unlawful" and "illegal"?
One means "against the law" and the other means "a sick bird"!

How did the Joker keep a skunk from smelling?
He put a clothespin on the skunk's nose!

What's the difference between a jeweler and the Joker in prison?
One sells his watches and the other watches his cell!

What did the Joker write near his ankle?
Foot notes!

How did the Joker fit a rhinoceros into his car?
He made one of the elephants get out!

Why does the Joker like biscuits?
Because they're both crackers!

Where can Robin always find happiness?
In the dictionary!

What does the Joker fill his car with?
Laughing gas!

What's the difference between a storm cloud and the Joker after a fight with Batman?
One pours with rain and the other roars with pain!

Why did the Joker try to paint all the cars in America pink?
He wanted to see a pink car-nation!

What's brown and furry, has four feet, a hump and lives in the Gotham City subway system?
A lost camel!

Why did they kick the Joker out of the flea circus?
He brought along a dog and stole the show!

What would Batman do if an elephant charged him?
Probably pay him!

How come the Joker got caught robbing the fast food restaurant?
He set off the burger alarm!

Why did the Joker throw eggs at the actor?
He thought ham and eggs went well together!

How does the Joker make a banana split?
He cuts it in half!

What happened to the Joker's green hair
when he jumped into the Red Sea?
It got wet!

What did Batman get when he dialed 555-273859361394364737 on the Bat-Phone?

A blister on his finger!

What did the man say after the Joker ran over his cat with a steamroller?
Nothing. He just stood there with a long puss!

What was the Joker's excuse for smashing the restaurant window?
He said he was on a crash diet!

What happened when the Joker robbed the hamburger factory?
Things came to a grinding halt!

What kind of bugs did the Joker send to some musicians to annoy them?
Fiddleticks!

What's the difference between the Joker's mixed-up deck of cards, a dressmaker out of glitter and a baseball player?
The Joker's cards are out of sequence, the dressmaker is out of sequins and the ball player is out to seek wins!

Why did the Joker chop up and give away all the trees from Robin Hood's forest?
He thought it was Share-Wood Forest!

Why does the Joker never discuss his secret plans on a vegetable farm?
Because corn has ears, potatoes have eyes and beanstalk!

Why did the Joker bring a motorcycle to Commissioner Gordon's office?
He wanted to drive the Commissioner up the wall!

Why did the Joker cross a mink with a kangaroo?
He wanted a fur coat with big pockets!

What kind of water can't be frozen by Batman?
Boiling water!

What did the Commissioner say when he heard the Joker had drilled a hole in the wall of police headquarters?
He said that the police would look into it!

What's the difference between the Joker and the Queen of England?
About three thousand miles!

What happened when the Joker blew up a boarding house?
Roomers were flying!

What does the Joker own that gets wetter
as it dries?
A towel!

Where did Bruce Wayne send his used
Volkswagen?
To the old Volks' home!

Why was the Joker surprised when
cucumbers grew from his ears?
Because he planted carrots!

Why does the Joker rob from the rich?
The poor don't have any money!

Why did the Joker cover himself in gold paint?
He had a gilt complex!

Why did the Joker fly to Metropolis from Gotham City?
It's too far to walk!

Why did the Joker feel hot after the baseball game?
Because all the fans left!

What did the Joker get when he crossed some cabbage with a tiger?
Man-eating cole slaw!

How does Batman subdue evil pigs?
He puts hamcuffs on them!

What did the Joker name his gallery of cow paintings?
The moo-seum!

What did the zookeeper say when the Joker sold him a sickly lion for $10,000?
"What a roar deal!"

What's the difference between the Joker and a boy's question?
One is a wise guy and the other is a guy's "why"!

How come Batman has a good driving safety record?
Because he is wreck-less!

What would Commissioner Gordon be if he sold bedsheets?
An undercover agent!

Has Batman ever hunted bear?
No, but he does do his crimefighting in trunks!

What did the Joker need to make an elephant fly?
A very long zipper!

What kind of party did Dick Grayson hold in the basement of Wayne Manor?
A cellar-bration!

What kind of bar won't sell drinks to the Joker?
A chocolate bar!

Where does the Joker fill his car's gas tank?
At the villain station!

What kind of tree did the Joker plant outside a drugstore?
A chemist-tree!

How did the Joker get a part in a horror movie?
He passed the scream test!

What did the Joker say when he met the Riddler's buddy?
"Any fiend of yours is a fiend of mine!"

How did the Joker attempt to divide the ocean?
With a sea-saw!

How did the Joker eat a computer?
Bit by bit!

Why did Robin freeze the Joker in a block of ice?
He wanted to see a really hardened criminal!

What did the Joker become when he boasted about his fighting ability to Batman?
A punching brag!

What's the difference between the Joker's jail sentence and a tooth with a cavity? *One is a decade and the other is decayed!*

What did the carpenter say after Bruce Wayne thanked him for fixing his house? *"Don't mansion it!"*

What kind of fish did the Joker bring when he wanted to borrow some books? *A library cod!*

How did Alfred the butler learn to serve spaghetti properly?
By using his noodle!

What's the difference between the Joker with a cold and Batman in a fight?
One blows his nose and the other knows his blows!

Why won't the Joker go bald?
He has a re-seeding hairline!

What kind of fight did the Joker start with Batman at the butcher shop?
A meat brawl!

What time does the Joker like best on his birthday?
The present moment!

Why does the Joker have twenty sleeves on his coat?
It's his coat of arms!

What did they call the thirteen cooks after the Joker hit them with sleeping gas?
Bakers dozin'!

Why did the Joker try to buy some teeth for a dollar apiece?
So he could have buck teeth!

Where does the Joker hide out when he's in Spain?
At his ha-ha-hacienda!

Why does the Joker always swim the backstroke?
He does everything underhanded!

What did the Joker say about the oatmeal they served him in jail?
He said it was gruel and unusual punishment!

Why did the Joker try to sell dirt to people?
He wanted to make grime pay!

Why does the Joker like to hear his doctor's jokes?
They always keep him in stitches!

What kind of fish did the Joker put on his peanut butter sandwich?
Jellyfish!

Why does the Joker's coffee taste like mud?
It was ground only minutes ago!

Why is it dangerous to play cards in the jungle with the Joker?
Because there are too many cheetahs around!

Where did the Joker weigh his pet whale during his train trip?
At the whale-weigh station!

What's the difference between one of the Joker's fake dollar bills and an insane rabbit?
One's bad money and the other's a mad bunny!

What happened when the Joker put a pile of foam rubber up his nose?
He got soft in the head!

Why did an owl make the Joker laugh?
The Joker thought it was a real hoot!

Where can the Joker always find diamonds?
In a deck of cards!

What did the Joker call the guy who kept a dictionary in his back pocket?
"Smarty pants!"

Why did the Joker rip up the rug at the theater?
He wanted to see the floor show!

How did Robin know the Tyrannosaurus
Rex was asleep?
By its dino-snores!

Did you hear about the Batmobile with wooden wheels and a wooden engine?
It wooden go!

Why did the Joker put wheels on his rocking chair?
He wanted to rock 'n' roll!

What did the doctor use to listen to the sneaky Joker's heart?
A stealth-o-scope!

What kind of monster did Batman throw into the washing machine?
A wash-and-werewolf!

What kind of tree did the Joker try to sell a chicken farmer?
A poul-tree!

Why does the Joker think Shakespeare wrote about him?
Because Shakespeare wrote, "To be or nut to be!"

Why did the Joker lock his soda crackers in the vault?
Because he wanted some safe crackers!

Why did the Joker bring his calendar to the bank?
He wanted to save time!

What did the Joker offer the dentist to drink?
A molar-tov cocktail!

What does the Bat-Computer eat for lunch?
Floppy Joes and Micro Chips!

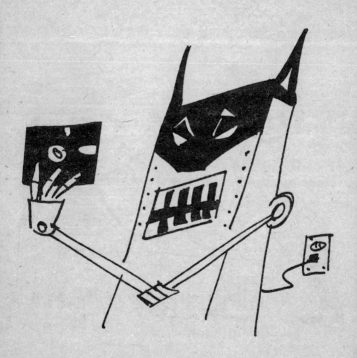

Why did the Joker call the policeman "Drummer"?
Because he was always pounding the beat!

Why did the Joker invite Batman to dinner on the roof of the restaurant?
He told him the meal was on the house!

What did the Joker get when he crossed a string quartet with a chocolate dessert?
Cello pudding!

Why can Batman tell an oyster his secret identity?
The oyster will clam up!

Why do the Joker's henchmen like to cook?
Because they get to beat eggs, whip cream and mash potatoes!

Why did the Joker run from the hungry lion?
He didn't want to become the mane dish!

What's the difference between the Joker and a wrist watch on the moon?
One's a lunatic and the other's a lunar-tick!

Why is doing nothing tiring for the Joker?
Because he can't stop and rest!

What game does Commissioner Gordon's country cousin like to play on the farm? *Crops and robbers!*

What did Robin call the Joker after the villain bit a policeman?
A law a-biting citizen!

What kind of fish does the Joker use to fix his piano?
A piano tuna.

What goes in white and comes out blue?
The Joker going swimming on a very cold day!

How come the Joker hasn't heard the joke about the bed?
It hasn't been made up yet!

How did the Joker make a bandstand?
He stole their chairs!

What does Batman take when he goes
into the desert?
A thirst-aid kit!

Why are Bruce Wayne and Dick Grayson's
tennis games so noisy?
Because they're always raising a racket!

What happened when the Joker couldn't
read his own handwriting?
He had to decipher himself!

Who was the dwarf detective who arrested the Joker?
Sherlock Gnomes!

What would Robin have been if he hadn't escaped the Joker's buzz-saw trap? *Shredded tweet!*

What did the Joker lose while running
from Batman?
His breath!

Why did the Joker tell the doctor he felt
like a broken window?
Because he had a sharp pane!

Why is a lollipop like the Joker after a
fight with Batman?
They both get licked!

Why did the donut shop close after the
Joker robbed it?
*The owner wanted to get out of the hole
business!*

What's the difference between the Joker playing the lottery and a country bumpkin?
One draws lots and the other drawls lots!

What's black and white and goes around and around?
The Penguin in a revolving door!

What did the Joker feed the elf?
Lepre-corn!

Why did the Joker scream when the tailor pressed his pants?
He was still in them!

What did the Joker give his snake
charmer friend to wear around his neck?
A boa-tie!

What did the Joker start when he threw a case of soda at Batman?
A fizz fight!

Why won't Batman give the Joker a dollar?
He doesn't believe in passing the buck!

Why didn't the Joker pay his phone bill?
He believes in free speech!

Why wouldn't the mailman let the Joker put the postage stamp on himself?
Because stamps belong on letters!

Why did the Joker hook up with his gang at the hamburger stand?
It was the perfect meating place!

Why does the Joker steal jewels and cars as well as money?
He was told that money alone wouldn't bring him happiness!

When did the Joker stop wondering where the sun went at night?
After it dawned on him!

What does the Joker have in his secret hide-out that allows him to see through walls?
Windows!

What can the Joker break with just one word?
Silence!

What kind of pie does the Joker make that sticks to your ribs?
A glueberry pie!

What does the Joker on a pogo stick have in common with the stock market?
They both have their ups and downs!

What does the Joker do when he can't get to sleep?
He lies near the edge of the bed till he eventually drops off!

How did the starving Joker eat a hot dog?
With relish!

What did the Joker say when he met a man with a wooden leg named Jones?
"What's the name of your other leg?"

What looks exactly like the Joker's eye?
His other eye.

Why does the Joker go to bed with fifty cents every night?
They're his sleeping quarters!

What goes "Ah ah ah ah ah ah"?
The Joker walking backwards!

Why did the Joker need toothpaste after a fight with Batman?
Because his teeth were loose!

Why did the Joker set Gotham City on fire?
So he could be the toast of the town!

Why does the Joker write his favorite gags on his sleeve?
Because he thinks it's his humor-wrist!

Why did Batman chase after the Joker when the villain stole a sausage?
He wanted to find the missing link!

Who does the Joker think were the first gamblers?
Adam and Eve . . . because they had a pair o' dice!

Why did the Joker put firecrackers in his pancakes?
He wanted to blow his stack!

What thirty-six inches in Glasgow does the Joker hate?
Scotland Yard!

How did Alfred the butler serve shrimps at stately Wayne Manor?
He stooped!

How did the Joker make an elephant float?
With two scoops of ice cream, root beer and an elephant!

Why did the Joker buy so many canaries?
Because they're cheep!

Why could the Joker never make a violin?
He doesn't have the guts!

How is the Joker like a retired school teacher?
They both have no principals!

Why did the Joker get hit in the face with
a lemon pie he threw at Batman?
It was a boomeringue pie!

Why was the Joker angry at breakfast?
His toast had gripe jelly!

Why did the Joker throw the composer in the bathtub?
He wanted him to write a soap opera!

What goes "Ha ha ha ha ha OUCH!"?
The Joker with a toothache!

What kind of candy makes the Joker tardy?
Choco-late!

How are the insides of a cherry similar to the Joker?
They're both the pits!

Why did the Joker drop a hatchet on the Batmobile?
He wanted to start an ax-cident!

How does the Joker say "eat" in French?
"Eat in French!"

What does the Joker call a six-pack of root beer?
A pop group!

Which of the Joker's crimes requires the most strength?
Shoplifting!

What newspaper does the Joker read to keep up on his fellow villains?
The New York Crimes!

Why is an old comb like the Joker after a fight with Batman?
They both have missing teeth!

How did the Joker make a hot dog shiver?
He covered it with chilly beans!

What kind of vegetables did the Joker steal from the jewelry store?
Carats!

What's small, purple and dangerous to every citizen of Gotham City?
A grape with a machine gun!

Does the Joker have any in-laws?
No, but he knows a lot of outlaws!

Why did the Joker ask the optometrist to fix his teeth?
They were his eye teeth!

When did Dick Grayson get a spell of mononucleosis, pneumonia and eczema all at once?
When he spelled them correctly in the school spelling bee!

What do many states have that the Joker doesn't want?
The electric chair!

What did Batman say to the three-headed monster?
"Hello. Hello. Hello!"

What are the spider webs in the Joker's hide-out good for?
Spiders!

How come the Joker doesn't like the joke about the ten-ton marshmallow?
It takes a lot of swallowing!

What did the Joker say after running over a kid's parked bicycle?
"Serves you right for parking it on the sidewalk!"

Why couldn't the Joker buy a suit to match the color of his eyes?
Because nobody sells bloodshot-colored suits!

Why did the Joker brush his teeth with gun powder?
He wanted to shoot his mouth off!

Why did the Joker swipe the parakeet?
He did it for a lark!

Is the Joker considered a picture of good health?
Yes, if the picture's a negative!

Why doesn't the Joker eat spinach?
Because he was told it would put color in his cheeks and he didn't want it to clash with his green hair!

Why did the Joker try to get some flowers for the Batman?
He thought it would be a good trade!

Why did the Joker leave Gotham City?
He couldn't take it with him!

How did the Joker avoid starving in the desert?
Because of the sand-which is there!

What did the Joker say when a cop told him he was driving his car over ninety miles an hour?
"Nonsense, I've only been driving for ten minutes!"

Why wouldn't the Joker write his clues to the Batman on an empty stomach?
A piece of paper would be much neater!

Why is it the Joker hasn't married yet, if he says he can marry anyone he pleases?
He hasn't pleased anyone yet!

Why was the Joker nicknamed "Scuba" in school?
All his grades were below "C" level!

Why is the Joker tall, thin and green-haired?
Because if he were short, fat and long-nosed, he'd be the Penguin!

Why did the Joker give up tap dancing?
He kept slipping into the sink!

What makes the Joker fast?
When the food in prison is too awful to eat!

What goes A B C D E F G H I J K L M N O
P Q R S T U V W X Y Z slurp?
*The Joker eating a bowl of alphabet
soup!*

Why did the Joker pull the rope across town?
Did you ever try to push one?

What do you know when the Joker has a sausage behind his ear?
That he ate his pencil for breakfast!

Why does the Joker have holes in his socks?
How else can he get his feet in?

Why doesn't the Joker use mothballs to get rid of moths?
He can't aim those tiny mothballs to hit the moths!

Why is the Joker a featherweight fighter?
He tickles his opponents to death!

Why hasn't the Joker ever gone water-skiing?
He's never been able to find a lake with a slope to ski down!

Why did the Joker paint a grin on the wall of the restaurant?
He wanted surface with a smile!

What room in the Joker's house has no windows, walls, floor or ceiling?
A mushroom!

Why did the Joker fire his gun at the electric fan?
So he could shoot the breeze!

Where did the Joker see dancing hamburgers?
At the meat ball!

How can Batman tell if there are elephants in the Bat Cave?
The floor is covered with peanut shells!

What does the Joker call a man who shaves twenty times a day?
A barber!

What came out when the Joker put a lead slug into the store vending machine?
The store manager!

Why has the Joker never visited Washington?
Because Washington has been dead for years!

What song does the Joker sing at Christmastime?
"Deck the halls with poison ivy, fa la la la la . . ."

What did the Joker say when the judge found him innocent on robbery charges?
"Does that mean I can keep the money?"

What happened when the Joker lit a match under the foot of a plastic surgeon?
He melted!

What kind of clothes does the Joker's lawyer wear?
Lawsuits!

What has one horn, gives milk and goes "Ha ha ha ha ha!"?
The Joker in a stolen milk truck!

What would you call the Joker in outer space?
An astro-nut!

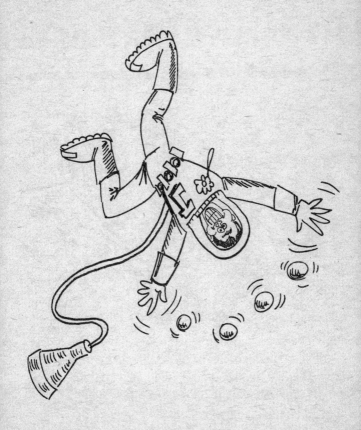

What illness did the Joker catch from the martial arts expert?
Kung flu!

How does the Joker get satisfaction?
He steals it from the satis-factory!

What's the difference between a bee and
the Joker?
*One's a stinger and the other is a
stinker!*

Why was the Joker shot out of a cannon?
To prove he was a man of high caliber!

What did the Joker get when he crossed
one of the Penguin's canaries with one of
the Catwoman's cats?
A peeping tom!

What's the difference between a phrase and the Catwoman?
One has a pause at the end of its clause and the other has claws at the end of her paws!

Why is a worm in a cornfield like the Joker listening to an anti-crime lecture?
It goes in one ear and out the other!

What does Robin have that's yellow and always points north?
A magnetic banana!

What did the Joker get when he crossed poison ivy with a four-leaf clover?
A rash of good luck!

What did the Joker say to the Egyptian?
"I don't know your name, but your fez is familiar!"

What goes, "Ha ha ha ha BANG!"?
The Joker in a minefield!

How does Batman prevent itches from biting insects?
He doesn't bite any!

What has green hair and purple feet?
The Joker stomping grapes!

What would happen if the Joker swallowed his knife and fork?
He'd have to eat with his fingers!

What's another name for the antique grandfather clock in Bruce Wayne's study?
An old-timer!

What did Batman say to Robin before they got into the Batmobile?
"Robin, get into the Batmobile!"

How does the Joker know when he's not wanted?
When they take down his picture at the post office!

What did the Joker get when he ate uranium?
A-tomic ache!

What's the proper name for Alfred the butler's special shish-kabob?
Shish-ka-robert!

Why did the Joker call the skeleton a coward?
Because it had no guts!

Why is Batman good for nothing?
Because he won't accept rewards!

What has green hair and a trunk?
The Joker with a suitcase!

Why did the Joker park his car in front of
the fire hydrant?
Because a sign on the hydrant said,
"Fine for parking"!

What's black and white and red all over?
The Penguin, blushing!

Why didn't the Joker cross the road?
He didn't want to be mistaken for a
chicken!

What has four legs, is purple and flies?
Two pairs of the Joker's pants!

Why does the Joker have green hair?
He'd look silly with blue feathers!

Where does the Joker get his hair cut?
On the ends!

How come Batman doesn't like to talk
about the 288 robberies the Joker's
pulled so far this year?
Because it's two gross!

How many different masks does Batman wear to work undercover?
Disguise the limit!

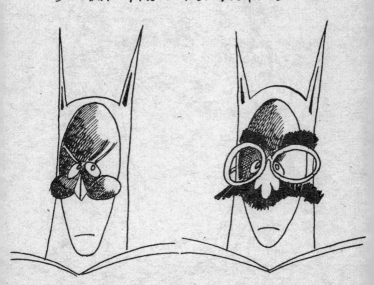

BATMAN-- MASTER OF DISGUISE

What did the Joker say about his experience with a werewolf?
It was hairy!

What walks on its head all day?
A thumbtack stuck in the Joker's shoe!

What kind of shoes did the Joker make out of bananas?
Slippers!

What kind of coat does the Joker put on only when it's wet?
A coat of paint!

Why was the Joker always getting in trouble at the cowboy ranch?
He wouldn't stop horsing around!

Why was the Joker's trained crab arrested?
He was constantly pinching things!

What did the Joker do with the trees after
he chopped them down?
He chopped them up!

Did you hear the joke about Gotham
City's smog?
Yes, it's all over town!

Why is the Joker good at giving Batman a
hotfoot?
Because the Joker's his arch-enemy!

What has green hair, three legs, three arms and seventy-five teeth?
The Joker with spare parts!

Why is the Joker's pen mightier than a sword?
It's a poison pen!

When is the Batmobile not the Batmobile?
When Batman turns it into a driveway!

Why does the Joker hang Venetian blinds in his hide-out?
Otherwise, it would be curtains for him!

What did the Joker get when he crossed a swimming pool with a movie theater?
A dive-in movie!

Why did the Joker bring a rope to the ball game?
To tie up the score!

Why didn't the Joker think the joke
about the germ was funny?
Because somebody spread it around!

What did Batman call the Joker when the
villain kidnapped a city in Pennsylvania?
A Pittsburgh Stealer!

What did the Joker get when he crossed
a banana with a bicycle?
A banana with training wheels!

What goes from Metropolis to Gotham
City without moving?
The highway!

What did Batman do when the Joker stole a hundred spring mattresses?
He sprang into action!

Why did the Joker try to spray Batman with gold paint?
He thought it would be a nice finish!

How did the Joker find the train with the jewel shipment?
He cleverly followed its tracks!

What did the Joker get when he crossed a thousand cars with a grape?
A traffic jam!

What does a 5,000-pound bat say?
"SQUEAK! SQUEAK!!"

Why doesn't the Joker allow elephants in his swimming pool?
They can't keep their trunks up!

What did the Joker get when he crossed an elephant with a jar of peanut butter? *Peanut butter that never forgets, or an elephant that sticks to the roof of your mouth!*

Why didn't the Joker like the joke about the Academy Award? *He didn't get it!*

What gives the Joker the power to reach the top of tall buildings with a single bound? *A non-stop elevator!*

How sneaky was the Joker when he looted the bowling alley?
It was so quiet you could hear a pin drop!

How much dirt is there in a hole the Joker dug to trap Batman, if it's ten feet wide and twelve feet deep?
None! There is no dirt in a hole!

What did the Joker get when he crossed
an elephant and a kangaroo?
Great big holes all over Australia!

What did the Joker get when he poured
hot water down a rabbit hole?
A hot, cross bunny!

How did the Joker keep an elephant from
smelling?
He tied a knot in its trunk!

In Gotham City, who can hold up a car
wth one hand?
A traffic cop!

Why did the Joker feed his plants dog food?
He wanted to grow collie-flowers!

How did Batman talk to the giant gorilla?
He used big words!

What did the Joker get when he crossed a dog with a monster?
A neighborhood with no cats for miles!

What art hangs from the ceiling of the Bat Cave?
A bat-mobile!

Why does Batman bring two pairs of tights when he goes golfing?
In case he gets a hole in one!

How did the Joker know it was raining cats and dogs?
He stepped in a poodle!

What did Batman and Robin do when they heard about the kidnapping?
They woke him up!

Why was the Joker upset when he only got half an egg?
He didn't get the yolk!

What did the Joker get when he put his dog in the bathtub?
Ring around the collie!

What did the Joker feed his pet monster for breakfast?
Scream of wheat!

Why couldn't the Joker's pet snake talk?
It had a frog in its throat!

Batman was driving the Batmobile without his headlights on. There was no moon in the sky and there were no streetlights on. An old lady was crossing the street. How did Batman see her?
It was morning!

What's the Joker's definition of an igloo?
An icicle built for two!

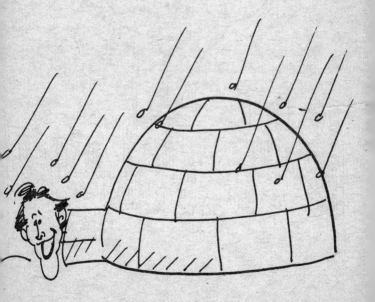

Who is the gangster from Maine who terrorizes Gotham City?
The Lobster Mobster!

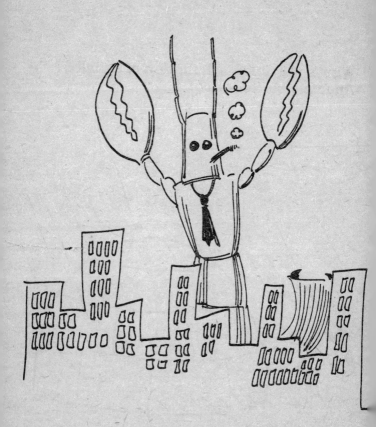

Where did the Joker wind up for stealing
shellfish?
Small clams court!

What belongs to Batman but is used
more by others?
His name!

Are bats sound sleepers?
Yes, if they snore!

How did the Joker get the farmer angry?
He got the farmer's goat!

How does the Joker file an axe?
Under the letter "A"!

Why did the Joker take a ruler to the restaurant?
He wanted a square meal!